Barf
and Dubai

[Stories of Skyscrapers and Sundowners]

by Echo

INDIA · SINGAPORE · MALAYSIA

Dedication

"Many many thanks go to friends and family in the making of this book. They know who they are and the depth of my appreciation.

This book should also recognise those, particularly those from southern and eastern Asia whose efforts and sacrifices have made modern Dubai what it is."

Preface

This is not a travel book or a celebration of brunches. Nor is it judgmental of the melting pot, Dubai. In truth, it is about what has always been the case for the ancient port city of Dubai. It only seeks to observe on different levels; you may find some characters propping up bars around the city or some situations in the city related to the overall ambit of what humans get up to. It is equally relevant to take each story on its own merits, as a combined piece, or with deeper resonance – all depending upon the individual reader.

The reader can enjoy the hints of fable or mythology. The book can be read in any order as per the reader's choice. Step in for a brief moment and take what you see or need and simply move on – as the city itself moves on. If the book has a hero, it is perhaps not an individual, but that is best left for the reader to decide.

Contents

Prologue – Mynah Birds

The fountain plays on. Its full basins stepped up, briming, overflowing with cool glassy water, dark in the evening sunlight.

The fountain seems so plentiful, always running with a continuous spilling and gentle splashing sound. It does not look processed or run through with chemicals. Just a joyful desert equivalent of a babbling brook, seated in a city centre hotel terrace.

The Mynah Bird now comes to Dubai. Locals comment on the change in the city from the old days, 'now there are birds'. People bring wealth and wealth brings food and water for little birds. The Mynah Bird is known for its ability to adapt and mimic. It picks up sounds and words, even to the point of sounding human. It learns fast.

The Mynah Birds, with their bright yellow beaks and eye catching white flashes, have many cries and calls in Dubai. Cries that bring their friends to also drink from the fountain. They overcome their fear of the unknown depth of the water and quickly dip their beaks. Just a quick dip of desalination and chlorine, then off again with a determined screech to hotel lights and pergolas.

The wealth of Dubai is all around. It is made obvious for rich and poor alike; a sports car here; the world largest, longest, tallest something there. It attracts all types, from all across the world; São Paulo and Shanghai, Nur-Sultan and Nairobi. Who can resist those Downtown lights?

However, the wealth that greets them is not as easily available as the water from the fountain. The little birds know that if they want to dip their beak, as they certainly are thirsty, their feet will get wet. Still, they drink and call their friends to come. The temptation, or the tragedy they leave behind, is balanced on the glittering sheen of the fountain they find in Dubai – and the different temptation or tragedy that may lie there.

Part 1 – Among the Boulevards

Among the Boulevards

It was the voice that carried to every corner, no amount of muzak or DJ bar music could stop it. It was a little-known frequency especially reserved, held in safekeeping by those men who came from the west of Scotland and had seen it all. It was not an unpleasant or ugly sound. In fact it had a roundness to it that made people sense leadership and confidence. There was a definite accent, but no lack of comprehension – unless you were just hearing the sound and not listening to the message. Women were attracted to it. There was a far-back tone and richness that made you think 'velvet' not 'cotton'.

Malcolm - never Malky, but no one dared ask why - was an imposing person by any standard. Over 2 metres tall, broad-chested and well-proportioned, Malcolm carried no fat and took no prisoners. There was the characteristic Scottish intensity, he always paid full attention to who was speaking to him, and that inquisitors light could bring a difficult cross-examination. That Malcolm was direct was not unusual, but of course it was part of his downfall. Despite the pseudo-colonial intonation he had developed, Malcolm was really a boor and a bully. This was subliminally communicated by the consistent slight tilt forward of his neck. This meant his large and completely bald head was always a little closer than you wanted it to be. Malcolm devoured cigarettes in the bar with face-caving elongated drags, plumes of smoke and flamboyant waves of his arm.

Many women in Dubai, and especially those from the Far East, found all this, combined with his ability to speak authoritatively on any subject, showed masculinity and power. The sonorous tone and, for the petite Asian women the exotic timbre of the words and phrases, only added to the presence of his commanding physique; he was a boss.

Malcolm's downfall was the message, although he never thought about it. What message are you sending drinking rum and coke washed down with lager every day? A hard-drinking 'work hard, play hard' kind of a guy? This was not a character fault in itself, in fact it was something of a survival mode for many in the city, but Malcolm always had aspirations for the bigger and better things that were possible in Dubai. The assumed approach worked well in Malcolm's late twenties and early thirties, when he was on the ground and the city started growing fast. It still had an edge of rawness, a corsair of the desert was useful, if not hard to find. However, the city had moved on - Malcolm had not. The message he conveyed, for all its clubbable resonance, was littered with innumerable curses and profanities. So self-assured and dexterously were they delivered you would think that it did not matter, just a normal speech pattern for the Brits. The locals did not see it like that. The older generation tolerated what they cared to translate and took Malcolm's usefulness on face value. The new, Harvard educated, generation found reason enough to ignore, then deride and eventually develop a hidden contempt for him. Malcolm was actually his own worst enemy.

Arriving in Dubai when it was a waning oil city, he had impressed with his energy, leadership and 'get things done' attitude. Now, a quarter of a century later, that gap in sophistication found him marooned in the desert of middle management. He would while away afternoons and often nights on a high stool with his cronies and the latest acolytes. Occasionally they were joined by bar girls who were tolerated, if they were engaging or attractive enough to justify a seat at the bar's high tables. The group was ever-changing, but Malcolm was always there, providing advice – seen it all, done it all.

" Look, I've been married four times. You're a good-looking woman and you just need to make a decision. Is it 'he's just a bit of fun and a good shag', or is it 'time to get a bit more serious'?" asked Malcolm almost patiently. Sam - never Samantha, that was reserved for her mother and, when he was really irritated, her father - was a couple of years into life in Dubai and passing thirty she was quietly becoming more anxious about finding a 'proper relationship', as her mother liked to call it.

"It's complicated." she pleaded. "He's not English, he's not even European, and I don't understand where it's going and how I feel.". Eyebrows raised, the incredulous gaze of cross-examination was fixed on Sam. Malcolm tried to choose his words carefully, "I told you. After four divorces I know, it only comes down to deciding if it's just a good shag or a day at the garden center. Look, there is a story for every person in this bar. Do you think I care about them? They don't care about me. It's just a boulevard of broken dreams darlin', get on with it.". Warming to his theme Malcolm pushed on, as ever, " It's not 'complicated'. A shag or the garden center. You're a good-looking woman, you can choose.".

Sam looked away perplexed. With some barely hidden condescension and no little arrogance Malcolm explained in his own style, "It's a melting pot interested in only one thing. There are one million Emirati's and they have wealth and a good life, maybe the best in the Gulf. There are two million expats, and some have a much better life than others, certainly most of the westerners do. Finally, there are seven million guys and girls on a contract, maybe in a camp, and they signed up for a better option than they had back home. In fact many of the guys are more marriageable now than they could have imagined because of it. Do you think they indulge in your 'humming and hawing'? Do it, don't do it, but do us all a favour don't mither about it".

Pints of lager were squeezed on to the high table and, as it was 'happy hour', a double rum and coke appeared, unrequested, but apparently welcome. Malcolm started into some of the 'hard luck stories' from over the years.

———— ❧❦ ————

1. Thursday Was Friday

Jack was a disappointment to Malcolm. When he was first in Dubai they had immediately been in competition in business and that continued even to this day. Back then they would have a couple of drinks and 'sort things out', who got what work - it just made life so much easier for all concerned. Nowadays Jack was, in Malcolm's eyes, a crumpled mess. He was so weak, he's seen more fight in his girlfriend's cat. Sure the nights with two beers and some sensible organization had faded away, but there had been the phone call or a quick coffee at the Irish Village, now even that had disappeared. Malcolm felt no small pain because of this. He couldn't understand why Jack didn't see the benefit for all in the old arrangement. For Jack life had moved on, not always for the best of course, but there were some things he could still control – like who he spent time with.

> The bar is full at first glance. A younger crowd, mostly white, mostly European, actually Brits & Irish on a weekend spree. A lot of young women with too little clothing for this country and too much to drink already. "Nothing wrong with that", some may think.

> Among this confusion sits an older guy on his own, trying to get some attention from the bar

staff; thick neck, crew cut, fading black t-shirt – no drink yet; no friends, colleagues or new acquaintances either. His fifty-eight years hung heavy. Jack tried to remember a time before the divorce when this had been enjoyable. When there was optimism for the future.

The bar noise and music swirl around and it's just about possible to be heard. A well-gymed forty-something, pretending to be a thirty-something, a little off-the-shoulder jumper and clearly no bra, is yelling in the ear of a disinterested broad-chested hulk of a man. Surely that's not a face-lift? Could it just be Botox? Her skin stretched across her face, it just doesn't look quite natural. She jumps up and down in an animated fashion. The bench-press hulk is not looking, or listening, the t-shirt is as tight as the botoxed skin.

Frazzled staff agree the main bar is full. There are no tables available, although yet more people tip into the clamour, the music and the card machines constantly beeping. The late arrivals are ordered, with confused and disappointed obedience, into the back bar to jostle amongst the pool tables while the real party is somewhere else. Some rebels break ranks, complaining to the Nigerian security and insisting on joining the party, a lucky few spot friends, colleagues or acquaintances. The rest are casualties to disappointment. Clothes fit where they touch. Drinks are bought, sunk and spilt. For some unfortunates there is a need for a rescue mission and a skilful steer to the safe harbour of a seat, others are simply swept along by their friends as their sea legs start to fail them.

Another well know tune with a bold, shoutable hook kicks in and the jack-in-the-box girls are up, arms aloft in a palm-tree wave of excitement, again looking for that attention. The guys continue to concentrate on their drinks and belittling chat about the previous night's victims. It is impossible to talk across the table, but you can shout if so inclined and many do. Conversation runs mostly side-to-side, projected into receptive ears and for that it always looks clandestine.

In the corners there are other stories at play. Some girls are in similar attire, but just don't have the look of Dundalk or Doncaster - it's more Dnieper and Dushanbe. A bulky Turk slow dances with a raven-haired Volga girl in a white jacket. There is no interest in the actual music. It suggests they 'get a room', or perhaps something financial is involved. It's a quiet darker moment untypical of the roar of enjoyment for big nights in this Irish bar. They are too focused on their own play to worry about palm-tree arms or jack-in-the-box choruses; just their sullen, knowing courtship and the delayed inevitable.

Solitary in the storm and shadowed intrigues, the man with the thick neck and black T-shirt is an island, his face deeply-lined with experiences and issues of other life times, but his eyes alert.

He tries again to attract any waiters attention, himself now standing, trying a Lisburn "Hey, you!". Still standing, plaintive palms come out at his side, but the gesture is unseen. He sits, looking around with a 'how did it come to this?' expression. That thought flitted through his mind again, somewhere along the line he had become detached from the regular social malaise. This was a connection he sought to recover, but also why he was relieved to depart all the sectarian complications of life back home. Now, to his surprise, he is even detached from the 'accept anything' world of expat Dubai. He is dismissive of the girls opposite and takes in the manoeuvres in the Donbas on his left flank. Is that what he wants, what he needs?

Disconsolate Jack's bespectacled gaze fixes on something sadder in the middle distance. His body remains hunched as if carrying a heavy stone, awaiting another pint of lager at some time beyond his middle distant trance. His thoughts are not of the empty apartment in JVC, but what went wrong in Belfast. The son who has no interest in him, the divorce, there it is again, the bloody divorce. However, it's more 'whatever happened to all those hard-earned wilderness years'. Fleeting time spent in what once seemed interesting and glamorous locations, that in truth no one has any interest in 'back home'. Jack grimaced realizing, once again, Almere is not Amsterdam, Batam is not Beijing, Pittsburgh is not Paris. No one cares about the tensions, the personal slights, the flies, or the hours lost awaiting early morning economy flights in provincial airports. Certainly his wife, ex-wife, never did – damn the divorce. It had come to him in his local, their eyes would glaze over, conversations were curtailed and eventually a few seemingly innocuous barbs, but actually cruel enough. He peered out at the confusion of humanity before him, yearning for a friendly cuppa more than 'love you long time'. He wondered where and when it stopped being good for his ego and where 'home' actually was. It's Thursday night, he's in a bouncing bar. He remembers a drunken comment of his colleague in Onslow, "Just remember, just remember, once you are over the hill you begin to pick up speed.". He feels like he's spinning down Mount Errigal on a push-bike without brakes. Those guys in Oz were all divorced, sometimes many times over. They didn't seem to care. They were all happy enough on big bucks, driving their 'ute', bitching and laughing in the camp 'smoko' every night. It didn't matter to them that it might as well have been Mars. Back then the money was good and you just had to keep some discipline, keep the head and focus on the money. Damn the bloody divorce.

Jack's thoughts were exploded with 'It's raining men. Hallelujah. Amen'. "Clearly a religious experience" he quipped out loud, but unheard - except to an appreciative audience of one. He admired the palm-tree appendages and smiled at his own wit. He tried an old favourite, thinking, 'That which does not kill us makes us stronger.' On a roll, he persevered with his disco inferno. As the temperature, and the torment rises, Jack reminded himself that 'without music life would be a mistake'. There is no wry smile this time. Where does that fit with the shower of men and the painful solitude? Solitude was meant to be a blessing. Jack watched the increasingly irregular and haphazard behaviour from the greater collective. It appears random, but is only so because of his distance. For them, together, they have a purpose, living life, oblivion or at least to dance along with it. For him, his dancing days seem long gone.

---

2. A Dimmer Light

Clients come and go, but over the years Malcolm had several dealings with Ayid. It had never been anything big and always seemed alright, but Malcolm was left with that feeling that somehow there had been a greater advantage for Ayid. He just couldn't work out how.

It didn't matter, it was well to the east of Kars. Ayid was running over his childhood in his mind, he seethed and reflected 'All the men there are macho, with all that macho shit'.

Big cities are a honeytrap for poorer regions. Everyone knows this, that the bright lights are not really so bright and often they don't shine brightly for you. "In the big city you will need to fight, or at least be ready to fight.", Ayid did not just mean struggle, or to work hard, that was just part of the whole thing. Ayid's father was so poor he begged for bread on the street. This is an experience that can mark a person. In the telling, in anger or sadness, it can even rest in the memory of children. For some it's just a step to a greater lack of shame.

For expats and Emiratis in Dubai this may all seem far away and in the distant memory of grandparents. Indeed it really is just under their nose, although not many look too closely. The millions of migrant workers in the UAE bridge the gap for millions more of their families in the Indian sub-continent and south-east Asia.

Day on day they tolerate the shared accommodation for mature husbands for months on end. Sometimes temporary or semi-permanent as labour camps. Sometimes permanent in barrack blocks of rooms in remorseless rows. Laundry dropped over the walkways, to describe them as balconies would suggest an architectural feature of bijou refinement, the sweat, the piss, the embarrassments of sexual frustrations. Yet in India and Asia, and increasingly from Africa, these migrant workers are seen as wealthy.

This sometimes extends to the point of 'millionaire' status, feeding and clothing the greater part of their extended family and owning property. Ayid had travelled far. He knew it is by trick of fate that some arrive as sons and daughters of northern boiler stokers, while others are the sons and daughters of those that can only house them under a worn out polythene sheet.

Meanwhile, seemingly unlimited wealth is enjoyed under the eyes of these migrant workers, who are in one situation, proles; in another, princes amongst their peers. How cruel and fickle fate can be? The crisp white traditional kandura, the sports cars, the expat expectations, the overpriced dining experiences. These things are beyond them. They are meaningless compared with care for the people who are the focus and weight of their responsibility, three thousand miles away. Meanwhile, they rub along in camp life. Ayid thanked his luck, the hard work of his father, and looked ahead to his next conquest.

---

3. The Old Red Shirt

Malcolm dipped his head, laughed, then shook his head. Steve had just walked past his high table. There had been the customary nod, but no conversation. For Malcolm, Steve was beneath contempt. When Malcolm had 'let him go', Steve had hung on to the dream - working on a local salary.

Awakening to the sound of racing Lamborghinis and in his mind singing 'Swing Low', Steve grunted at the irony and wondered, could it be the city is a little quieter for Christmas Day? He was glad to get his Bengali boss off his back. He knew he had done his job ten times better than him, but in family companies there was always family politics. More important to Steve, he just couldn't be bothered looking for another job or possibly leaving Dubai. The fact it was Christmas meant zero to Steve. He got his bonus, which got smaller every year, the new boss was away shagging his Filipino secretary in Fujairah for two days and he could kick back with a few cold ones. Thank Christ he wasn't trying to get back to the Midlands. What was waiting for him there? Only drab boredom, aunties and cousins, 'Alright!'.

'Underneath the glamour lies the emotional disappointment, the stress and the impact of not re-connecting within families and within generations in western Christian cultures', this was the kind of bullshit you heard on do-goody BBC Radio 4. It was not important for Steve, just noise from a place that is no longer home and didn't understand. Christmas and New Year were for kids and grannies. He was beyond it. The only function for him was everyone wanted a holiday and this was as good an excuse for one as any. The lads got pissed up and the girls got a bit friskier. He didn't care about baby Jesus or the angel Gabriel. He knew it was just a story to keep the populous in check and focused on something other than what was really going on - the gathering and manipulation of power. He knew what those guys in Davos were up to.

Steve liked Dubai. It forgave his advancing years. It allowed you to do whatever you want - if you had the money of course. Sixty-one year-old western men with twenty-one year-old Filipino girlfriends; or just friends with benefits. It didn't matter to anyone else here. Neither Dudley nor Dublin, it was another world, with an extra degree of separation from all those conventions back home. Steve liked that, it led him away from convention and expectation.

Steve knew the real toil was mostly accounted for by the millions of migrant workers, but he didn't care much about that. It's just the way it was, and probably always would be. He was not going to change it and had no intention to either. He wasn't one of those do-gooder politically correct cheerleaders, saving every broken-pawed rabbit and their lost cause. The price for him was working his 6 days for 60 hours per week and putting up with his boss's bullshit. 'Work hard, play hard' had always been his way.

Now wide awake and rummaging around to make tea, he laughed as he calculated how much richer he would be if only he had dropped one pint of Guinness off each night's tally. That would be enough to retire to Thailand, not just the occasional fun week in Bangkok. The hair was pretty much gone now, the waist was thicker than it needed to be, but he still enjoyed the big nights at the Irish bar when they came along. He still dug out his Lions shirt from fifteen - or was it sixteen - years previous when the tour came on. He could still bore the arse of any Irishman with tour stats and stories of tours he had never seen. In fact although he could have afforded it, he had never been on one, but then who was counting and who cared – it was Dubai.

---

4. Jumeirah Night Moves

What was it about this guy? Every time Malcolm bumped into Ayid in a bar he was accompanied by the most desirable women. Ayid always introduced them for a brief hello and they were always different; sometimes from northern Europe, the Far East, central Asia, the eastern Mediterranean and slightly more often than not his home country. It always seemed to be friendship, never business, for Ayid. Malcolm quietly seethed a little. The emotion made him more than uncomfortable.

Nothing to say, nothing to do but drink your beer. After sex with fifty women, and all that 'friends with benefits bullshit', the world didn't seem such an entertaining place. Ayid had let his bile build up and he always regretted it. That second glass

26

of Scotch from that heavy glass bottle with those Egyptians had been a mistake.

Sure the music pumped on and the bar always had more or less people ebbing in and out, but how many were interested or interesting? Did he seek solitude because in that he could reach for something else, or that he just couldn't be bothered anymore? His mid-life had begun and he hadn't even noticed. Another pint of beer for a start, was simply that; no great adventure. What was he waiting for? His next call for work? His next assignment; more dry days, lost days, rosters revolving and changing.

At least the women changed over to something older and more familiar. Some men were seeking the euphoria of long ago coming of age, or shared big nights out. Their emotions fuelled by guzzled pints of lager, overpriced whisky and shots. Ayid turned his head away. 'What was this?' he thought, was that just a touch of jealousy he felt, or was that arrogance? He had seen there behaviours before, too many times.

Maybe he also longed for those late nights as the centre of attention, with his old friends drinking too much and talking too much; great days he realised now. Those nights in his old home city, so far away, the girls who always seemed to be around and, for him, always available. He had learned early on that he was a catch, with an obvious source of high income, the owner of the business and a man who other men liked to follow. Broad-shouldered, confident, handsome, with a more European facial structure that made him stand out in a subtle way that women like to read. His quieter, more self-controlled posture and body language indicated an unflappable cool head and only added to the mystery and intrigue. Now he sat alone with his beer and others shrieks and laughter, meaningless music and disappointment.

On the adjacent table sat a foursome. Two lads, a couple of likely-looking van drivers from Dagenham. Callow and barely men at all, they were a sartorially-challenged, a slack-jawed assembly of bad haircuts and gangling limbs. The two girls opposite had consulted on attire. Peach-patterned diaphanous stretch, newly bought, hung from one and clung to the other.

One boy-man was more confident than his supporter. He sat beside Clung on their bar stools. From time to time his arm stretched confidently across her waist and his hand rested nonchalantly on her large backside, without objection. Constantly tugging down her dress, Clung shrieked with laughter at every sentence. Ayid wondered, could it be that all sentences this boy-man shouted over the music were hilarious?

Looking into his beer and glancing disinterested at the sport on the overhead televisions, Ayid considered, Was this it? Was this the abyss? Was this really the oblivion to be desired? The two boy-men could not believe their luck and nervously fiddled with their peaky sweeps. Meanwhile, in the wash-room Hung and Clung planned their night moves. Ayid had also seen these behaviours before. The nervous bravado between the boy-men, the tactical retreat for consultation and make-up checks.

Again, what was that emotion or sensation he felt? People, men and women, sitting alone at bar tables or high stools was not uncommon in Dubai. Everyone was between something, waiting and looking for the next thing. Constantly, compulsively, nervously mobile devices were drawn and checked for messages - hopefully leading to greater enjoyment. It was rare to see someone speaking in to these gadgets, but rarer still to see them out of people's hands. Like a grown-up comfort blanket, they made people feel important and connected. For those sailing on a bar stool life raft they were a lifeline. Ayid joined the party and consulted his phone.

5. The Ballad of the Moon-Faced Girl

The taller central Asian girl with the round face always sat on the diametrically opposite side of the bar from Malcolm, hidden by the spirits and the optics. He had spoken to her once, but only once. It had been disconcerting and troubling for him. Her face was expressionless as she skilfully managed and then blocked his attempts at conversation. She seemed oblivious to the crowd of curses, but it wasn't just that she could look straight through him – more, she looked into him. Those long rain sodden Sunday afternoons with Uncle Hugh in the tenement flat with its dated care worn furniture. "Malky, Malky, pass the ball. Not like that, like this", then later, "Malky, can you make tea.". She sipped her pint of lager beer through a black straw. He remembered how the conversation finished. She looked up from the straw and into his tortured memory. Was he aware his left eye wrinkled, perhaps twitched, as he took a long last drag? Somehow he realised that her knowledge and experience trumped his four divorces, but for Malcolm not those Sunday afternoons with Uncle Hugh.

> Unable to take the isolation of another night of four walls and definitely not wanting to spend any time with house mates who looked down on her, the Woman decided to sip beer through a straw in a hotel bar. She was taller, with an hourglass figure, more so than was usual for women from Central Asia. One of those countries ending in 'stan', where the Chinese and Mongolians blend with Turkish and European

peoples. The countries that four generations before had accepted a communist revolution, but also held to their faith at first and then each following generation had become less and less committed. She wore western clothes and drank her beer sip by sip. The English pub hidden in Dubai was a well-known location, with heavy wooden fittings; carved, fluted and corniced as in a church. The lighting was also dark and dimmed further as the night wore on. It was early in the week and the quiet bar found the Woman talking on and off to Jack, while the Keralan barman flitted around. Jack welcomed the company, there weren't many like her back in Belfast. The Woman drifted across where she had lived in Dubai and the difficulties of her virus blighted employer. Jack mentioned he was divorced, she smiled in that faint far eastern way – politely, but knowingly.

At that, and as it was quiet, the Woman started to tell a story of a first marriage. Jack listened but always had the feeling something was lost in translation; was this her first marriage?

The Girl in the couple was young and more western in physique than usual, her face had the Asian look of the steppes. Her own mother had been even more noticeable in stature. It was fair to say men always fixed on her in a crowd. The Man was approaching middle age and newer in town. It seemed he had an important job with 'the Party' and now the government.

The Girl was impressed by his maturity and he took her to Party places and expensive restaurants – even the expatriate restaurants. These were places her friends could only dream of, weighed down by their mudhook adolescent boyfriends. The Man's connections and affluence were apparent. The Girl was flattered and beguiled by him.

Several weeks passed with the couple under a watchful eye and the Man always respectful and patient. Each in turn became relaxed in the other's company. One day, in the heat of the summer and in a new summer dress, the Girl and the Man took a walk into the country. It was an obvious, pleasant and innocent enough way to idle away an afternoon. Eventually they were miles from any house or person, under the big blue sky of central Asia.

At first it seemed like a caress, but soon it was too rough and the Girl became uncomfortable. She tried to push back, but he seemed ready for that, the Man's body was already tense in anticipation. Then fear gripped her. She started to plead with him. She fought harder to break free. His hand went over her mouth and as he pushed her to the ground the Girl was struggling just to breathe. Again she wriggled and writhed and tried to shout and scream, but muffled by his strong hands of course no one could hear her. When she neared exhaustion the Man forced himself on her.

The Girl knew it was rape, the Man knew it was rape, but he didn't seem concerned.

The Girl sobbed. He chatted as if nothing unusual or revolting had taken place, almost like he'd seen it all before. She remembered the sound of his voice, but not what he said. She remembered her guts churning and the bruises on arms, legs and shoulders - the smell of him, the heel of a strong hand pressing in her cheek, the fat fingers over her mouth.

Afterwards they carried on as if nothing had happened, only that the Girl avoided being alone with him. Her friends admired her 'catch', chiding her for how cool she was with him. The Girl's parents were quietly satisfied that such an important and well-connected person should pick her, although the mark of her beauty, as that of her mother, made them talk with pride that it was bound to go like this.

Finally, the Girl picked her moment to confess what had happened to her mother. To her surprise the mother didn't flinch when she told her. Without expression she watched and listened as the Girl sobbed and cried again in that pain. Finally, when it was all cried out, in the still moment before the pain returned, the Girl whispered to her mother she was pregnant. Then, taking up her courage, she simply stated said she could not have the child.

Her mother looked at her for a long time and then firmly and dispassionately made it clear she would not hear of it. She was matter of fact, there are men and there are women - how special does she think she was? The mother reminded the Girl what a catch the official was, this was the way men were sometimes. The Girl's heart was stone, but she finally nodded acceptance that she should marry the Man as her mother insisted.

The marriage was a quickly-organised official procedure, with no cultural trappings and unusually few family members. Only two people made an appearance for the Man, one oily underling toadying after him and, distinctly separate, another man who was ages with the groom. This stranger stood ramrod-straight and had an old scar across the side of his forehead, which distorted his expressions. Both these witnesses left immediately after the formalities, in fact the festivities were curtailed and muted. With knowing looks some realised that the baby started to show. A few months later a healthy baby boy was born, but he was un-loved by the father, un-wanted by the mother.

After the first year, the married couple were constantly fighting, not caring when or where the bickering broke out. He was often 'away' on business. When at home, just sitting around drinking, or in town with his colleagues for hours in bars. Occasionally the friend with the scar appeared. He seemed slightly deferential to the Man. They were always very respectful to each other with formal handshakes and a lot of eye contact, as if taking a formal toast to remember and acknowledge something past. They never stayed to talk or explain, not even one shot of the much loved vodka passed their lips in the Girls presence. The old comrades always went to the same old bar in town. The Man would return late to sleep on the couch. Sometimes he did not return at all.

With the rape, the birth and the bickering, the Girl had become a Young Woman. She had got through and begun to take pride in her responsibilities. One day in the silence of the kitchen, she coolly handed the Man a letter. It was an official application for divorce. When he opened it at the kitchen table he dropped his head and gave a hollow laugh, which came out as a grunt. Then he picked up the vodka on the table and a glass. He fired down two shots and tried to laugh again.

He stood up pushing back his shoulders and then wandered around the house, picking up a few almost random things, his chess bag, a black and white faded photograph of someone in uniform, an un-opened vodka bottle, two shot glasses. He gave another grunt and seemed to gather more purpose. All the cash in the drawer was folded into his wallet - she knew it wasn't much - he tutted and shook his head. The Man picked up his winter coat, but no bag of clothes, no books, nothing from the bathroom. He put his hand on his car keys and paused for a moment looking straight ahead. Then he left and never returned. Two years later an official letter arrived saying they were divorced.

At that Jack tried to make a sympathetic noise, but it seemed futile. He had no need to speak, only to be there so she could speak. He was a little confused by his beer and how the story ran. Was the Woman speaking about herself, or maybe her mother, or perhaps even the grandmother? He consoled himself that it was often difficult to guess the age of people who had something of the Far East about them. The Woman reached for her straw and took a sip of her beer, waiting for the barman to busy himself. She started again. There was more to follow.

The Young Woman, after some years, met a second man, a Quiet Man, one who seemed incapable of rape or anything so terrible and terrifying. He seemed quiet and considered in all things. She liked his introverted nature, no drama, no chest puffed-out, no mysterious friends with un-explained scars. He was from the other side of the city and a good neighbourhood. She was comforted and reassured by a greater familiarity with his nature and his local preferences in simple basic things that were closer to her own, besides he seemed to be natural with her son. He was not a big drinker, but enjoyed coffee with his friends at the market.

The Quiet Man would listen to their stories and poor jokes of those too old to come into town and would sell their local fruit and vegetables. He would drive around and buy from them at a pittance, and each morning he would sell what he could. However, he did not seem to have a good head for business, always forgetting to add the cost of his fuel, his pitch, the bribes to secure the pitch, or buying poor quality produce to sell. His profits were small, but this did not matter to the Young Woman. She had the house and he sold just about enough for them to eat and pay the bills, she was content with something that seemed normal enough. The Young Woman knew she had no need for bright lights and big dreams, she had flown close enough to that flame already. She lived with the Quiet Man, she had re-built her confidence, there was a second marriage and in time she fell pregnant again.

On the day of the birth there was great pain, then the medicine brought some calm. The Quiet Man had gone outside to wait. After several hours and no birth he was told he could go home. He left his number at the desk and went home to wait with his coffee; clearly she wasn't quite ready. No call came for him to return, but the baby did, a girl. "What a tragedy." said the receptionist on the phone, following underlying complications there was surgery and the Young Woman had died. He took the new baby, his daughter, to the grieving grandmother and asked her to take care of the funeral.

Sitting in the kitchen with his coffee he realised he felt relieved. He realised he had always been an unwilling father and now he was a widower with his own house. He realised he had also been an unwilling husband. The revelation brought a glow. He had been hi-jacked into a marriage and fatherhood. He nursed the coffee in his hands, in his kitchen and mulled things over, 'The house. It was a good house, on the edge of town, suitable for an important official – indeed a desirable house.'. He finished his coffee and decided on another cup. The Quiet Man thought to himself, 'What an opportunity.'. Yes, he could leave some money with the grandmother and head off for a new future further west - better opportunities and better weather. A flicker of a smile came over his face. It all made perfect sense to him. He could sell the house to that realtor who was always asking about it and be out of here in no time. Only his clothes were really his, all the other junk could go to the grandmother. By lunch time the next day the bargain had been struck and he set-off back to the house to collect his few things and head off for a better life.

When he got back to the house he could smell his coffee and hear the grandmother clattering about in the kitchen, 'Clumsy old bat.' he thought, 'Who did she think she was with all those twinsets and curves? Marilyn Monroe?'. He was stunned in silence to see his wife, the Young Woman, who had just given birth, sitting at the table, a coffee cup growing cold in front of her. He kept silent. The grandmother asked knowingly, "Why did the realtor call me?". He remained silent, but couldn't help wonder what mix-up or mistake happened at the hospital.

This time there were no fights, arguments of controversies. The Young Woman coolly handed over the official letter filing for divorce. The Quiet Man simply left the house and went to see a lawyer. More years were lost, but this time it was not matrimonial but legal disputes that burned up the time. Sure, the second husband had disappeared, it was thought toward the Black Sea, but that was the problem. His lawyer was always full of excuses that he could not reach his client. When on occasion he did write back the second husband's lawyer always asked the most nonsensical legal questions, 'Can you prove you were married?', 'Is it correct that the divorce can be processed in this city?', 'Did you abuse your husband?', 'What is the value of your combined property?', 'Of the value what is the proportion of moveable's on the day of filling for divorce?'.

So it went on for one year and, tragically, two years. The Young Woman was now the Mother of Two, a son and a daughter and two divorce settlements to deal with. The husband's lawyer came in person with a detailed list of what he wanted from the contents. The Mother of Two conceded everything just for it to be over, at least she had the house and of course the legal bills. When the lawyer left she was numb once more.

The Moon Faced Girl sighed and sipped her lager beer through a straw. Jack stared at the Woman incredulous, a rape, a property theft and it seemed there was still more to tell - and he was still not sure who owned this story. As the telling now wore on the tone of her voice was sadder than the two divorces and the physical and mental harm. The two earlier fates once survived seemed cause for a celebration of resilience, but she remained curiously un-emotive and objective.

Of course several years of child rearing and struggle followed for the Mother of Two, but as there are men and there are women, another man came into the life of the Mother of Two. He was kind and thoughtful and never asked for anything or coveted possessions. They needed a car, he got a small car, not too big not too small. They thought about day-trips, they went to the mountains. They took lots of walks and improvised barbeques in the countryside. The little boy and girl played in the mountain meadows among the pasture flowers and the adults talked and shared bottled beer from small cups.

The Mother of Two had been hesitant and steadfast on what she wanted to do and when; children first, everything else second. She never slept with the Kind Man. When necessary she shared a family room with children and often the grandmother. The Kind Man knew her story and accepted whatever she wanted and how she wanted things to be. He often returned to the city only to come back soon after to bring them home.

Eventually, after two spring seasons, as the warm air of summer blew in, the Mother of Two suggested the Kind Man could move into her house. The Kind Man hesitated and asked her to think carefully. She smiled and knew her gambit had been returned. Three weeks passed and over tea from the samovar they agreed that he would move in, the weekend before the first trip to the mountains for the summer. Everything was as the previous year, the children played in mountain meadows, the grandmother tended the barbeque and the adults sipped their beer from small cups. Exceptionally, the Kind Man and the Mother of Two shared a room, but not a bed.

Jack now intrigued was a little surprised and saddened at this, but asked that they drink one whiskey to cheer the spirits. The Moon Faced Girl smiled, as if remembering another better time and glasses of Irish Whiskey appeared via Kerala. Jack took a proper nip, but the Moon Faced Girl twisted the moulded crystal pattern between her thumb and index finger. Jack couldn't help himself, "...but didn't it work out". The Mother of Two and the Kind Man never married, but lived together for many years. The samovar provided tea. The grandmother visited less, but encouraged more children. Their bed was a safe place, so they laughed and shushed the grandmother, but, unlike the summers in the mountain meadows, no more babies came.

Jack was a little stunned as he sat in the dark surroundings. The Moon Faced Girl looked resolutely into his eyes and said, "Don't you know a tragedy always has a sad ending."

Intermezzo – The Siren Song of Isha

Is this the most beautiful sound in the world? An eerie but certain sonic resonance. There is no need to listen, just to hear.

At nightfall pleasure yachts silently hover into the dock at the Marina. Soft ripples of water catch the reflections in the dark. The myriad lights in amber threads at the shadowed harbour side and as jewels of white, crimson and gold bedeck the gently drifting flotilla. They ornament the night and humbly gild the song that reverberates from another world. It transports all and the call is all-pervading.

The sound is welcoming then captivating, without edges or interruptions to its constant flow. Your surrender to its presence is unconditional. It echoes with echoes upon echoes, soaring around the mirrored towers of glass and steel, unsuspecting shining minarets.

The sound, a glissando reflection that replicates to great and greater, high and higher effect. As the grace of the moments in harmony pass, each slight decay followed with simple charm by a more exquisite and fascinating note, at once delightful and delightfully more alluring.

The sound, is a spiritual in the seventh night of Ramadan. One simple man does good for all to conjure up this departure, a delicate but dazzling incantation; an aria on the warm air

Feel the Isha rise, rise up; rise up.

Part 2 – Adrift in Dubai

1. A Land Full of Strangers

"Janus, give this Helot some of your wine.". While Janus passed over his goatskin bag, Cleomenes looked around the high pasture. The goats were halfway down the hill toward some small trees and bushes. There had been a Messenian village here in years gone by, *Abudi*, but now it was an unwelcome memory and long overgrown. "No Helot, not a sip, drink your fill." commanded the Spartiate. Pan knew that the place of a Helot was to pay close attention to his master. Slaves are best served by silence and doing what they are told. He took another, longer, drink. The sun was high in the day and he had been chopping wood all morning. The undiluted liquid hit his stomach and he regretted the wine he had drunk earlier. "Don't you think this is a particularly pathetic Helot, Janus?" sneered Cleomenes.

Janus took a good look at the Helot. Certainly he was dirty, his hair and beard bedraggled, his tunic frayed and old. However, "pathetic" was not the first word that came to mind, perhaps 'tough', 'lean' and, dangerously for the Helot, 'proud'. Cleomenes had decided to take a long walk with him that morning. As his most useful free man, Janus had the job of supervising the Helots, but they were spread over a large area. Janus had seen Pan on a few occasions before. He kept to himself, often deliberately sending his wife to the city. The other Helots seemed to mark him out for respect. Once Janus had seen two Helots seek out Pan up here on the mountain.

In truth Janus was wary of Cleomenes. He was volatile and moody in his youth and this was not changing with age or responsibility. He didn't like being his man to keep an eye on the Helots. He knew he was simply Cleomenes' spy, feeding his paranoia. It felt thankless and demeaning for a free man Perioikoi. He quickly blanked that thought from his mind, hoping his face had not given anything away. He would much rather have spent time in the foundry. He got a lot more out of that work for his family and for himself, with more respect in the city for that than as a labour master. Of course the Spartiate's still looked down their nose at him. They would never soil their hands with foundry work, but the hoplite warriors needed their weapons and that usefulness automatically brought respect. That was the case with Cleomenes' father and for that Janus could almost have called Cleomenes' father a friend. They had been at war together and worse still, in Janus' mind, they had also been at sea together and even fought shoulder to shoulder on the deck of a galley. After this terror he had sworn to Cleonmenes' father he would always support the son, given sacred offerings on that oath, and now he was happy to be on dry land.

Cleomenes said he liked these tours because it stretched his muscles and built his resilience to the heat. Janus always walked the route beforehand, but Cleomenes often threw in something extra. "There's just so many of you and you all seem the same." mused Cleomenes, "Seen one Helot seen them all. What do you think Janus?" the Spartiate was unusually talkative today and Janus felt a tension. Usually there were only clipped instructions and one-word requests. Janus had noticed that ever since he had left the hoplite agoge, Cleomenes had become more frequently sarcastic and insufferable, somehow with a slight uncertainty that he covered with these displays of confidence, actually misplaced arrogance Janus thought. On such occasions Janus observed that he hated and baited the Helots more. He baited his own Helots the most and Pan was such a slave. Janus knew now he needed an appropriate answer, "Pathetic" he repeated.

"No, but this one is particularly wretched. Take another deep drink Helot." Cleomenes reprimanded. Both Janus and Pan looked at each other, each mind spinning and calculating who was in more trouble. The Helot knew best. "What is your name Helot?" asked the Spartiate. "Pan" the Helot replied quietly, instinctively seeking to intone some deference and respect, he may be proud but he wasn't stupid. Cleomenes clicked his neck, feigning patience. "What? I can't hear you, Helot." Cleomenes growled, "Drink Helot. Again, what is your name, your name?". Pan wasn't sure what to do first. He quickly took a drink and said clearly "Pan, master.", then bowed his head. Janus sighed, perhaps in relief, and moved as to suggest they should walk on. The Spartiate did not move, he clicked his neck on the other side.

Pan had felled a tree and was making kindling with a small axe. The sun fell directly down upon them. Pan was already too hot and needed a break, the sweat and heat in him was just below boiling. The axe now lay on the ground next to the kindling and the large rock on which Pan had been chopping the sticks. In one smooth motion Cleomenes picked up the axe and spun the shaft in his hand. It was a deft movement, not unexpected of a trained and experienced hoplite. He felt comfortable with this tool. He spat on his hand and rubbed the shaft into his palm. The axe was well made and the weight of it felt good for him. He ran his thumb over the edge of the blade. It was still razor-sharp. Cleomenes looked at Pan with momentary appreciation. He kept the axe keen, more like a weapon.

When Cleomenes was sixteen he had been left on a mountain with only such a tool and his dagger. Cleomenes had to sharpen both the axe and the dagger well. On pain of humiliation or worse, he accepted his tasks. On the mountainside he had made his own kindling, lit a fire and snared a rabbit. That night a mountain lion came round. He could hear it, maybe even smell it. The lion's shadow mixed with those cast by his fire. It was hungry and Cleomenes needed to stay awake all night in case of attack. In the half-light of dawn, as the fire finally dimmed, the attack came. He felt its approach, he was not tired, he was ready, all senses were alert, his hearing helped anticipate it. The old lion rushed forward, but Cleomenes instinctively threw the axe at a downward angle and it sank cleanly into the lion's skull. Afterwards, he had burned the lion's heart and some of the meat as an offering. Then he took the skin back to the agoge. He was chided and chastised for this trophy. It lacked humility and suggested bravado. Cleomenes in this thoughtful moment forgot both Janus and Pan, who were staring at him, "Drink Helot, drink!".

In the heat Pan was starting to feel his stomach turn over. The rough wine was moving through his blood and he was sweating more than he should. "Look at him sweat Janus. It's just like a sow." Cleomenes had a mocking tone. "Like a sow." repeated Janus dutifully. Cleomenes spun the axe. At that moment two figures appeared at the edge of the bushes. It was Pan's wife and daughter. They were a good distance away. Instinctively they were rooted to the spot. Cleomenes noticed them and smiled wryly. "Ah, Helots that grow out of the ground. How many Helots are in Sparta Janus?" asked Cleomenes almost absent-mindedly. "Many more than Spartiate's." answered Janus too quickly and then immediately adding "I think this one works hard for you." attempting a casual response. The Spartiate now looked intently at Janus, "Drink." he growled at Pan.

Cleomenes spun the axe. "This is a particularly good tool." he observed, "The blade is sharp, and it is also well-balanced. Could this be of your making Janus?" "Perhaps.", replied Janus. He knew it was because of the shaft, "Let me take a look at the head for my mark." Cleomenes ignored him. He was staring at the Helot.

Pan looked confused and a still greater sense of apprehension came over him. His stomach was now churning and the sun was insufferable. The axe spun and Cleomenes said light-heartedly, "Sing the hoplite marching song, Helot." Pan's face flickered a wrinkle of frustration. Everyone in Sparta knew this song, but only the hoplites and their wives ever sang it.

While the captive Helot hesitated, Cleomenes asked Janus again, "How many Helots in Sparta, Janus?". This time Janus knew he needed to be more straightforward, "About seventy thousand.". "And how many fellow Perioikoi, Janus?" countered Cleomenes instantly, knowingly. "About twenty thousand." answered Janus flatly. Cleomenes looked down in feigned reflection, "And how many Spartiate's?". "About ten thousand," answered Janus quickly, trying to satisfy the questioner and end this game. "And that's one too many." mumbled Pan, who fell to his knees, puked, retched and puked again – sweat glistening in the sunshine.

Cleomenes heard the comment clearly. He clicked his neck. He looked closely at the Helot, his emotions cloaked. Janus knew it was time to pay attention to his superior, who still spun the axe absentmindedly. "There's just so many of them. They create a land full of strangers." mused Cleomenes quietly, but loud enough for Janus to hear. In the distance the wife and the daughter remained where they stood, rooted. They still held the wild rosemary they had gathered. Wrapped in its fragrance, they intuitively had the wisdom not to interfere. "So, seven times more than the Spartiate's." said Cleomenes to himself.

At that point the Xenoi, Aco, came over the hill. He had been in Sparta since the start of the summer, trying to promote trade. Janus knew the worth of this outsider. He also had some helpful ideas for the foundry. They had been trying some experiments together. In addition, he knew what was happening outside Sparta, which always fascinated Janus. Cleomenes was at best circumspect about Aco; so much to say, never keeping his own counsel, blown in from the north. True he had knowledge of many skills, of the seas and far off lands, but he always seemed to have a better way than the Spartan way. Worse still, he was never slow to share it. Cleomenes held up his left hand to acknowledge Aco, but also to stay his advance and most importantly to keep him quiet. He looked directly at Aco, "A land full of strangers." he repeated clearly for Aco to hear. The axe spun, "Take a drink Helot and sing the hoplite marching song." Cleomenes the hoplite said firmly. Aco looked on wide-eyed. Pan took an unwelcome drink. With his bile rising the sweat seemed to only gravitate towards his eyes, it stung. His head pounded. He started to sing quietly what was meant to be a rousing warrior anthem.

"Look at this Helot Aco." said Cleomenes in mock disgust, "What was your word for him Janus?", "Pathetic." replied Janus, the flat tone returning to hide his concern. Cleomenes continued, rising to his theme, "They take to strong drink, that they cannot hold and they wilt like dried leaves under the sun. Pathetic." Cleomenes spun his axe faster.

As the Spartiate and his trusted Perioikoi disappeared over the brow of the hill, the wife and daughter reached the Helot. The witnesses were all in shock as they realised there was nothing to do. The women kneeling by the slumped body clutched each other in tears. Aco removed the axe from the Helot's temple. More blood came out, but soon it was only a trickle. After some moments just staring at the scene he cast the hatchet into the dust, disconsolate. Then he motioned to give the women a small bag of kindling and some coins. Aco tried to shoo them away, whispering assurances that he would take care of everything. The women looked back at him; suspicious, uncertain, adrift. Finally the mother took the bag and the money and pulled the stunned girl away. In the distance was the faint sound of Cleomenes laughing and then a distant, but distinct refrain of the hoplite marching song.

2. Formerly the Continental Hotel

"War is not romantic. There's nothing romantic about children lying dead on a roadside."

Volunteer, Ex-British Army

Ayid took in the scene, his raqi inspired hangover was almost at the point of bearable. It had been a good night, but he couldn't forgive his friends just yet. He gave thanks his stomach was ok, but oh, his head – he was simply hanging. There was a pool-side buzz despite the continuous beats of the DJ's messages to the speakers. These messages, assaulting the ranks and rows of sun-loungers and sunshades that surrounded the pools and jacuzzies. Even by early afternoon most of the spaces were taken. Additional entertainments were in progress.

He surveyed a mixture of bare-bodied relaxation and alcohol-fuelled partying, all performed by adults, no children, who sought some downtime, some me-time, or simply some distraction – but not a classic Dubai brunch, too formal. The idea was relaxing while in a party atmosphere. The usual Dubai premise, that you can have it all - simultaneously. The Sun Worshippers and Partiers relaxed, as groups of gossiping friends popped, bobbed and minced in a fashion not too aggressive to be dancing, but in a restrained and grinding way that suggested an even greater dance talent for the poppers and the bobbers – even if imaginary. Occasionally absent-mindedly studying each other's partners - more so if apparently un-attached. All this was performed in various states of undress, down to swimming trunks for men and bikinis for women that was more lingerie than swimwear. No worries, it was fun and distracting.

There were tangoing stilt-walkers from east of the Vistula, two fabulously-dressed bottle blond dancers who gyrated and posed progressively around the sun-loungers and a middle-aged circus unicyclist juggler in purple lame waistcoat. Coolest of all was the beyond-barrelled Hawaiian-shirted saxophonist in white plastic sunglasses. He skilfully stretched, noodled and panted away over the club beats in a meaningless but persistent fashion. More than a few pounds over, and most likely never handsome in a way only a mother could love, the radio mic allowed the pasty sax-man to also wander amongst the revellers or relaxers. The Sun Worshippers and Partiers alike took their chance to selfie themselves with the costumed promenading bottle-blonds and rasping and gasping sax-man when they came by, and even seeking them out if not so handy. "Are we having a good time? Hell, yes, of course we are!", Ayid wasn't sure. He needed something to eat and wished he had brought paracetamol. When would that sax player finish honking? Was the sun brighter today or was it just him?

The drinks flowed, the music drove on, and each sun-lounger and gazebo played out their own social malaise. The groups of tattooed expatriates laughed and nodded while on their mobile phones. Occasionally an eye-catching individual would want to be noticed, like the baseball-capped blonde with twigged fingers dancing for the benefit of her own sun-lounger.

More complex was the perfectly-made up Persian Princess, wrapped in her own aura for all to see. Her clearly-enhanced behind, now self-consciously, even for her, needing a diaphanous scrap to cover it. Her right buttock being allowed out provocatively and, of course, knowingly. It seemed to be an augmentation fashion of the moment. The breasts looked good, as she knew, and not to the point of disbelief. The ass is fair game to be any size, 'bigger is better' was the fashion at the moment. Was it her son or her lover who could not settle on any activity, not even cool stillness? Ayid observed this cameo from behind his shades hoping to take his mind off his desperate need for sleep and a chemical rebalance.

The real champagne was out for the Persian Princess and the friend who joined them, all three together on one large gazebo. The son, or lover, or daughter drank pints of cold beer. They restlessly dipped in and out of the water, sometimes drinking, sometimes in animated conversation, sometimes looking off into the distance as only the beautiful ones know how. She constantly plagued the African service attendant for minor chores and necessities to enhance their gypsy encampment between the pools. The Persian Princess occasionally allowed the beats to move her although it was clear she did not possess natural rhythm.

It was noticeable that few of the tracks had any effect on some of Sun Worshippers, the Emiratis or other non-European expatriates - no nodding, popping or bobbing. The Europeans however, motioned their heads in time when the moment took them, then self-consciously repeated the exercise to emphasise it was deliberate and cool - even if they were the wrong side of forty for it ever to be cool. Unless, of course, you were the sax-man. It was a great feature of Dubai, no one cared what age you are. Everyone was free to play along with the party, so long as they looked good – man-mountain or Persian Princess. The heat, the sunshine and the light made everything seem completely normal – big ass, big biceps, what's not to like? Ayid felt trapped in a dehydrated nightmare. He seldom popped or bopped and certainly wouldn't today. He took a walk into the cooling water of the pool, but swimming was out. He caught himself staring at the Persian Princess, but failed to snap out of it.

Two thousand eight hundred and ninety seven miles to the north west, under the sombre spring sky of a godforsaken Ukrainian oblast, the same mobile phones recorded different movements to different beats. Everything was captured in frighteningly high-definition hand-held clips. In the city the splendour of the former Continental

Hotel was now just a smoking mass of twisted steel and blackened rubble. On the edge of town, more like space troopers than fathers, heavily-equipped soldiers lift three year-old children over taller galvanised road barriers; each as if weightless - all this as incendiaries pepper them. Desperate grandparents, dehydrated, dirty, bewildered, trying to hurry along a sodden roadside. Could it be that the temporary ceasefire would be a lie? That they could not escape their home, their lives, their memories? Could they not have, at least a temporary reprieve, some basic needs, safety, a wash, some food?

At both the poolside and the reception centre the burgers await eager hands.

---

3. Gimlet's Revenge

'I am the man to rule the world' beat the international club tracks prophetically. The March heat was building. Between the walls of the terrace and the bar, now renewed with bar stools, a group had arrived, mostly lads and some slender, younger and impossibly pretty Slavic girls. The lads and their groupies, established their camp in this space at the middle of the bar. Some of the lads were already heading towards a good quota of alcohol for the evening and their extrovert personalities couldn't be helped. Every passing girl was stopped with a comment or a sweaty hug they definitely didn't want. Some tried to match wits with the guys, depending on their dexterity with English.

They were a mixed bunch. One of the lads, curly-haired and Mediterranean, could have been from Manchester, Marseilles or Marrakech. He looked around gimlet-eyed as the alcohol started to soak into his system. Perhaps tonight was one for fighters, not lovers. Even when pissed he kept his own counsel. He looked towards the prettiest Slav, to check if she was happy enough. It took more than a moment to focus. A flicker of recognition and he turned back to his drink. Others in the group could have more certainly been of Arabic descent, perhaps Algerian, more probably Egyptian.

Another lad, an obvious exception and the one most clearly four sheets to the wind, declared himself to be German. From first glance there was no reason why that wouldn't be true. He certainly looked Bavarian, with his diminutive beer bulk and kiss curls. His accent, using excellent English, was still stubbornly Teutonic. His diatribe eventually arrived at the exclamation "What is your name? Come and join us.". He listed from left to right. As the pupils set in cornflower-blue retina telescoped in and out it was not clear who or what he was trying to focus on. Maybe just the next piece of stimulation, the next victim of his bastard file wit and dubious charms; "I'm Ali.". "Really? Short for Alasdair?" interrupted the camp Filipino barman. "No! What would I want to tell you my real name for!" he spat dismissively.

There is always one guy who is pissed first, causes the most trouble, falls out with his friends, needs to be rescued from drowning in the ladies washroom, scraped off the pavement, or dragged from a supportive bar at 4am. "We go everywhere." he proudly boasts, miming the downing of an imaginary stein and completing it was a Germanic click of his tongue, "Toc!". The man who never wanted Oktoberfest to end, but now spews in Sports City rather than Schwabing.

He may have been the schtein, the jester, the tolerated one, but the captain of this crew appeared to be Egyptian. Taller than all, broader than all, brasher than all, he was the one who set the pace. Stopping all comers, young or old, male or female, with questions or antics. Some targets, of Arabic culture, simply froze and blocked him with clearly well-chosen phrases. This was probably for the best. Some of European background hesitated in their politeness, or even tried to match the Braggart and his new-best-friend bravado.

While Schtien flitted around resolutely annoying all comers, this Braggart touched all around them, balancing on the edge of charm, knowing everyone was out for a good time. That was the pretext and the cover for the behaviour. Elderly wealthy gentlemen, looking to relive happier times, tolerated him in their space and even enjoyed the forced laughter. Others just tolerated him, especially young women. He was the giver-of-unwanted-affection-in-chief, the hand on the elbow, the insincere welcoming but unwelcome bisé, and always the unwanted moist embrace of perspiration. His bulk and presence, combined with the crowded space, made it impossible for more fragile humans to do other than submit for a few seconds of intrusion. They hoped the hot, sweaty forty year-old embarrassment in a baseball cap would just go away, the story to be recounted as a great escape over cocktails later.

The Gimlet, however, had a girlfriend, the most arresting Slavic girl in the group. Immaculately flicked flaxen hair falling well below her shoulder blades. The highest cheekbones, an elven nose and most spectacular piercing crystall grey eyes. Undoubtedly this Tsarina could have stopped Russian tanks at forty paces, and she knew it.

She sat on the low wall completely aware of the power flowing from her chest-less charisma. Arresting in simple butt-high denim shorts and tied white blouse, a kind of perfection, or at least Gimlet thought this. The same uniform was worn by her handmaidens in attendance on either side.

However, what was the price for all this drink-fuelled excess? The Braggart was momentarily running low on entertainment. At first it was to be an intimate word, perhaps sharing something with the Tsarina that others in the group did not know about him, maybe the drunken tomfoolery was an act. Could he actually be sober and for once willing to share a genuine thought, perhaps a feeling? He took her head gently in his shovel hands and suddenly kissed her full on the lips. She tightened at the last moment, with an animal reflex she pushed him away. She firmly but quietly remonstrated with him.

The group took another step toward self-destruction and the Gimlet saw nothing as his mood grew sour. Harsh words of frustration were quickly and quietly hissed to the ladies in waiting. This was not the end of the matter.

---

4. Three Witches

Looking on from the bar the Egyptian casually wondered, 'Why were they here?'. The three young women were clearly from out of town, ok, so they are tourists, but even a Thursday night in the Irish Bar deserved and benefited from more effort than this.

The plainest had, as usual, mistakenly tried harder than her friends, but failed. The crop top was neither stylish, nor flattering – and she knew it. Her insecurity in this social situation was obvious. She asked herself, why had she chosen this when she was constantly trying to get her weight under control? She cursed the effort required and the expectations of such a glamourous city. The malice she felt was more intense than when she had at home. She couldn't help but notice the daily catwalk of sylph-like women, tanned, stylish and perhaps double her age. Worse still was any woman's crowning glory, her hair. For her it was a torment of crinkles and aging dye. Sometimes she just couldn't be bothered. She plodded on over nights such as these. This riotous racket that, in truth she was contemptuous of. So many people gadding about and gabbling nonsense. Her defences and insecurity did not allow the slightest contact and her scorn she knew would keep her warm. Longing to step out of this pressure and expectation, she twice cursed the unseen hand that held a mirror to her disappointment. Not for her the bunkum of the light on the inside - the world was an ugly place, full of ugly people. However, she knew her enemy and enjoyed the times with her coven. The laughs at others expense, the slights, the shared knowing looks debited to the account of their victims. It wasn't that she couldn't tolerate the pretence of going somewhere for a good time. To say that would be too obvious. It would give the game away. That's where the sweet chilled delight lay. She savoured it on her caked lips. Her mask of convention made her unwilling to give up participation, although she cursed this too - and had done so on many Tuesday nights in her back bedroom. Her greater fear was not that she was the wallflower, but that her two sisters in such delights would leave her there. If a man would take time over her, and they rarely did, her eyes would only be for her friends. Her slightly hunched shoulders confirmed her preference for nettlesome conspiracies over natural conversation. It gave the game away, if you paid attention. Her quick sidewards glances at whoever or whatever fell into her malicious eye. The delicious spite of it all.

The middle one, in student black T-shirt and canvas jeans, these black rags subtly hid a lack of style or aspiration. She knew, or thought she was worldly enough to know, that this look was always acceptable in an understated way. However, it owed more to midnight on a rainy Garnet Hill, than the prevailing permanent sunshine of Dubai. She was more confident, her head was up and her eyes darted around. Her confidence was of one more beautiful, but she wasn't. The body language confirmed her confidence was born of arrogance. Her reference was her perceived superiority of her hometown, of which she was of course mistaken, it should have been what she did not know about her current location. However, that did not concern her, only that its strangeness was worthy of contempt. Superior in her own mind, she liked what she saw in the mirror every morning. She believed that she was smart and desirable and that's all that mattered. However, it was also strange that not a single man in the bar ever spoke to her. This was a city where people strike up a conversation at a glance, even if it was always the same second language conversation. She enjoyed Crop Top's gossip and unflattering remarks. It never once occurred to her that no one spoke to her. Her own unflattering comparisons came from another darker jaded world. At home she would be more careful to keep her opinions to herself, but here, with the small reinvention of a new location, with her sisters – no one knew what they were saying if they could keep a straight face.

Black Rags looked towards the third sister. She was a different story. Black Rags admired her friend, if any of them were real friends, because she accepted her, or so it seemed. Cutty Sark was a dangerous beauty, with a veneer of innocence and of course she knew it. She also knew how to manage the power that came with it. Not for her lost time staring into the mirror to see what was not there. Not for her the endless selfies to boost an ego, only buoyed by the delicious amputation of pathetic unwanted boyfriends. The auburn spell of her fine poker-straight hair mixed with slim torso and elegant limbs and fingers. Her manner was of course natural but also self-assured, no need for her to be cocky or proud. Her movements were lithe, like a dancer. Men made way for her and allowed her in to the bar without question. She was always the subject of the eternal gaze and it was all the more intense in this environment. She was in her element. Again, dressed in late-period student weeds, but also with a more feminine touch, a terracotta scarf, a prettier top, light pedal-pushers –not heavy or out of place. She cast a spell around her that her two friends could only admire and sometimes covet. However, it was her face of course that confirmed her desirability. She observed as quickly as the other two, but with an ease that did not give the game away. Her features were finer, her nose was not snubbed, but long and delicate. Her cheek bones were high, but not protruding, the skin was unusually whiter, finer and colder. Her eyes sealed the deal, especially for any unfortunate men from the eastern Mediterranean who fell under their gaze. They saw everything, but had the hint of the intrigue of her inner self. This was the spell. The beery men were bewitched and some brave sailors rolled bravely forward.

The heavy-set Egyptian took the fourth bar stool at their table with a confidence in his ability to manage these situations. He greeted all amiably enough, but after the pleasantries he only looked at, or spoke to, her - Cutty Sark. The conversation was the same as ever. It always worked in Dubai and it was wise not to wander too far from the path; 'where are you from?', 'do you live here?', 'where do you stay?', 'are you married?'. Another good trick, introduce a friend. The friend is the best guy in the world. They have done everything together, you name it, such laughs and crazy times. The friends speak together in their first language. However, the trick is not on for tonight, the friend blows it. His wide eyes and features suggest something is seriously amiss. Not tonight the back slapping, the stories of desert forays, the shots upon shots and late nights in Deira. His reticence creates an unnecessary tension in the good time atmosphere. He is concerned about something and he cannot focus on his role as second. He is not interested in women tonight, even if they could be available. The sisterhood of course soaks in his lack of wit or charm for later dismemberment. The Second has some greater concern, his wife, his car, his rent, his visa? He stumbles, still wide-eyed looking off into emotional or financial oblivion. The Egyptian struggles to maintain his carefully crafted bonhomie. His usual surprise reinforcement has let him down and this has thrown him. He briefly considers what his friend's problem could be. The worst at the moment - the visa. Maybe the job – no job, no visa.

Crash-landing in unchartered territory, the Egyptian realises there is a third language skittering around the table. The incantations and spells of Bellshill banter he is struggling to understand. Most of it seems unspoken, a collection of looks and knowing glances. Amongst the flicker of cocked eyebrows and unfinished words he has an uneasy feeling. To try and recreate his safe place as the centre of interest he starts to order drinks, but soon finds himself well into three rounds of porn-star martinis and snacks. Another round of martinis and a small light dawns in the distance. Is it the T-shirt? Is it the shorts? Is it that he is maybe twice their age and heavy-set. He knows he is a little over-weight, but no woman in Dubai really bothers about that. On this table things are different. With the rear guard air-cover of another round of martinis, and a stick of Slippery Nipple shots, he engineers a retreat to the bar and the unfolding drama of his friend's marital difficulties, his malfunctioning car and his ever-increasing rent. His friend knows the Egyptian can do nothing about a visa. Back on safe ground the dirham has dropped. He can now pass on his own scorn, "Frigid Bitches".

Cutty Sark looks around smiling her invisible vulpine sneer that actually appears like it could charm the world. She lifts her porn star martini to The Egyptian and his panicking jobless wing-man, "Cheers" she calls in her final curse.

5. Dates in Al Barsha

The virus had led every nightspot to become an eatery. Masquerading under the banner of food and fun, the Good Red Song, or whatever the overblown karaoke bar was called, had a clientele of thirty-something expats behaving like twenty-somethings downstairs. Upstairs was more sparsely populated with a balcony.

Two African women appraised the scene and stroked the stems of their glasses of overpriced red wine. One Amazonian, with cropped hair and black patterned dress. The other, more petite, with a full Afro hairstyle, the bright white jumpsuit singling her out, luminous in the gloom. For them the night was moving slowly, the thin popular dance music stirred nothing in them.

Circling the venue was a tall heavy set and perfectly bald man. If there was ever a guy who looked like a serious heavyweight boxer, it was this guy. T-shirt and shorts, he clearly had made no effort for his night out, only swapping his flip-flops for trainers. He had been 'out' for a while, judging by the garbled English competing with the music. Each table of strangers was subjected to enquiries, even tables not keen to indulge in his collegiate bonhomie. Serge picked them off in no particular order, randomly resting his elbows where seemed easiest, shoulders forward, letting his presence impose itself on unwilling new companions.

Serge was on patrol with his friend, Alexander, and all the signs indicated that they were ex-Russian forces. Judging by the empty glasses, both had clearly been drinking in this venue for some time. Serge was not handsome, he was intimidating, bulky but not fat or obviously overweight. In fact from the massive shoulders which stretched his t-shirt, it was clear his stomach was tight. Why was he here is this lightweight student union night spot? Serge was Alexander's wing-man. Alexander was different. Of similar height, but by comparison, wiry and actually of more regular physique. His features were angular and sharper, not doughy like Serge, that striking sharpness that some Russians have. He sported close-cropped blond hair. He seemed a good ten years younger than Serge, but carrying less abuse it was probably five. He wore a casual, but neat, button-down light blue shirt and straight leg denims. Continuously on his phone with calls and messages, he paid little attention to Serge's monotonous shark-like circling, hunting for potential victims. Alexander was also restless, he stood up, he sat down, he stepped a few metres from their table and straight back with a new message. Slightly animated in how he held his phone, he used these small flourishes as if to justify the importance of the calls.

A few paces away the African girl in white jump suit started to become more tense, fidgety, now twisting her glass intently, drawing on her cigarette more deeply, releasing plumes of smoke as backdrop to their presence. Time ticked and now pinching the stem of her glass, she ordered another red wine for herself and her colleague.

Sensing the vibrations in the water, Serge made his move and two worlds collided. Several minutes of his charm passed between himself and White Jump Suit. He tried to bring Black Patterned Dress into the conversation, no interest. He explained their tables were close by, obviously looking to merge the party into one. No one made a move and Serge swung back to base in Novosibirsk.

A few minutes later a slim woman with waist-length blond hair, pink camisole and tight light blue jeans stepped carefully up the stair as if picking her way over bodies after a party. Finally she entered on to the balcony with her hair flicking back as if everything was beneath her. Alexander's prey finally seemed to be in full view. He immediately made a fuss about bites and vodka, arms were waved and waiters were commanded. A bottle was somehow spirited on to their table, the prey effortlessly moved into their company and on to her waiting stool.

Anna surveyed the state of affairs. She had seen Alexander before, in a more appealing state. This was not that night. She knew Alexander well, intimately. A slight disgust came over her. She shared some pleasantries with him, but for Serge only the minimum she could get away with. She had also met him too many times before. If tonight Alexander was a wayward child, Serge was a galoot – and a dangerous one at that. The problem was the feeling of unpredictability that hung around him every night. It disquieted Anna. He sensed her unease and to release the tension they both felt, he broke off on his circuit once again. She set her body for a clear signal; she was not looking for a raucous night with the boys. She refused the stick of shots that appeared and sipped her drink. Serge knew this passive hostility. Alexander did not bother. He had long ago concluded there was more shared experience between Serge and himself than women can understand, no matter how beautiful. The foxholes, the burned-out buildings and Serge's basic needs and wants.

On this pass of the venue Serge followed up on table Nairobi with a long stop-over. Further attempts at conversation were made and, to Serge's suppressed delight, this time the African ladies came over to Novosibirsk. Social awkwardness followed. The obvious and available seat was by the balustrade where White Jump Suit could sit next to Serge. Alexander on his left talked earnestly to an apprehensive Anna, who was now also trapped against the balcony. Black Patterned Dress quickly, and certainly more soberly, appraised the situation. After a few anxious and seatless seconds, a swift retreat to Nairobi followed. White Jump Suit took more than a sip of her red. She looked coldly straight at Anna; friend or foe? Anna's delicate, if hardened, features gave nothing away, nothing, not a flicker, not the slightest movement of torso or face.

White Jump Suit was what men termed 'fit'. She had a curvaceous slim figure deliberately accentuated by the Lycra material. Swaying gently Serge was as desperate as seven year-old for chat, laughs and companionship. White Jump Suit knew this, of course, so she set to work to weave her web. First, a few words of encouragement for Serge, then time to make sure she was safe with Anna. White Jump Suit confidently stood up, walked around the back of Serge and Alexander running a long spindly index finger over Serge's shoulders and, despite the virus, air-kissed Anna, just like they were old adversaries from the Bolshoi. It was a brief feline territorial moment. Sure, it was totally forced, false and fake, but Anna played along. She was more concerned how to get away from Alexander and cursing her poor judgement in coming out that evening. A few moments of polite, but stilted, conversation passed between the women. White Jump Suite returned to her stool, she was in position. Anna had a face like a smacked backside and, as Alexander buzzed in her ear, she only wanted to go home.

Black Patterned Dress had left. The lone African surveyed her quary. Leaning in she sought a more earnest conversation. Serge's left arm swung low, he in turn hunched forward to de-code her east African accent. His English was escaping him. The African woman steeled herself. She had known tougher nights than this.

❦

Epilogue – The Old Man from the Desert

"Chose your friends wisely and be careful what you wish for." was the counsel of The Old Man from the Desert sitting on his heals. The children rolled their eyes. Behind him the city sat in a glowing twilight relief as the wind dropped.

The Shamal that summer blew in drifting sands on the roads and a choking haze. After three days people were staying home and the late August heat hung around with a clawing and stifling persistence. The Old Man from the Desert smiled and would simply say it was good news, "The world has aired the carpets.".

Whirlwinds sometimes flare up in the desert and likewise in the city. They surprise and aggravate, starting up suddenly they are more than mischievous. Furniture slides around and cars pull over. The Old Man from the Desert would shake his head, frown and say under his breath, "The djinn Zairba'a travels tonight.". He knew Thursday was now Friday and, unusually, he spent those nights in his room silent and wreathed in shisha smoke.

The Shamal that winter was harsh. Strong gusts persisted and heavy rains came and went over three days. The modern roads were full of water, just as the drainage was full of sand. The modern city of the future was at a standstill. The Old Man from the Desert would smile to himself, chuckle and simply say it was good news, "The world had taken a hammam.".

Cold winds from the north-east occasionally come to Dubai. At that The Old Man from the Desert would always gather up his battered wooden backgammon box, take the children inside and the shutters would come down. He would mutter about his old adversary Pazuzu, demon of the ill-winds, their old battles in his youth, the new torments he now brought to the world and then he would say no more. Eventually an old bottle of clear liquid from Syria would be brought down. It instantly became opaque as he added water. The children looked on wide eyed at the trick and knew nothing more of demons, thankfully. He would drink one small glass quickly, drawing back his lips to display sand stained snaggled teeth and inhale the vapour to the back of his throat. Then the bottle disappeared, never to be seen again.

The Shamal was the third of that year and now in its third day. The children had grown weary of backgammon. Looking round with wide eyes The Old Man from the Desert would, with a seemingly absent minded benevolence, reminded them, "Those that seem bad are sometimes good, or at least trying to survive the same as everyone else. Some are just bad. We will never understand their malevolence.".

———◆◆———

79

Printed in Great Britain
by Amazon